This book belongs in the home library of

HARRY COLVILLE

For Lindsey – J.O.
For Elly and Molly, in the land of Oz – L.G.

OXFORD
UNIVERSITY PRESS

Great Clarendon Street, Oxford OX2 6DP
Oxford University Press is a department of the University of Oxford.
It furthers the University's objective of excellence in research, scholarship,
and education by publishing worldwide in

Oxford   New York

Auckland Cape Town Dar es Salaam Hong Kong Karachi
Kuala Lumpur Madrid Melbourne Mexico City Nairobi
New Delhi Shanghai Taipei Toronto

With offices in

Argentina Austria Brazil Chile Czech Republic France Greece
Guatemala Hungary Italy Japan Poland Portugal Singapore
South Korea Switzerland Thailand Turkey Ukraine Vietnam

Oxford is a registered trade mark of Oxford University Press
in the UK and in certain other countries

British Library Cataloguing in Publication Data
Data available

ISBN: 978-0-19-272746-6 (Bookstart paperback)
ISBN: 978-0-19-279172-6 (hardback)
ISBN: 978-0-19-279173-3 (paperback)
ISBN: 978-0-19-279208-2 (paperback with audio CD)

1 3 5 7 9 10 8 6 4 2

Printed in Singapore

THIS book takes its inspiration from the much-loved song 'Here We Go Round the Mulberry Bush': the words can be sung to the same rhythm and there are animal noises and actions, too. It's a book that invites lots of high-energy enjoyment but it's also a book that can be shared with young children to talk about habitats around the world, encouraging them to develop an awareness of the great diversity of wildlife that our planet supports. The book begins with animals you might find in a garden or on a farm. There are also animals from seashore, ocean, desert, rainforest, savannah, arctic and wetland habitats and the book finishes with a group of nocturnal animals in a night-time setting.

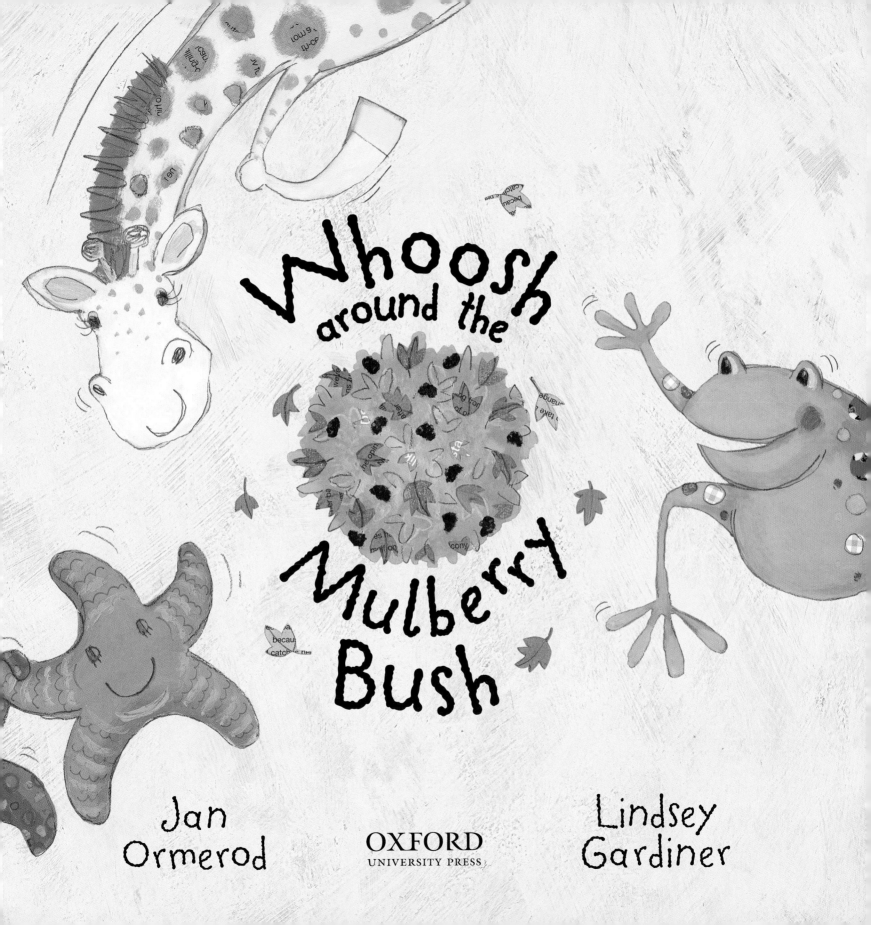

Whoosh around the Mulberry Bush

Jan Ormerod

OXFORD
UNIVERSITY PRESS

Lindsey Gardiner

Here we go round the mulberry bush, with a mulberry **whoosh** and a mulberry **swoosh.**

Here we go round the mulberry bush on a **cold** and **frosty** morning.

This is the way we slime along, flippety flap and sing a song.

Here we go round the **flower bed** on a sweetly smelling morning.

This is the way we **cockle doo,** **cluck** and **honk,** baa and **moo.**

Here we go round the **chicken coop** so early in the morning.

This is the way we **dig** and **dive**, **scuttle** and **crawl**, **nip** and **pinch**.

Here we go round the **sandy shore** on a breezy summer morning.

This is the way we flip our fins,
swim and swoop,
dart and dive.

Here we go round the **deep** blue sea on a **salty bubbly** morning.

This is the way we Sneak and Slink, YIP YIP YIP, woo woo woo.

Here we go round the **tumbleweed** on a **scorching** desert morning.

This is the way we clack and call, slither and squeeze, scream and swing.

Here we go round the **jungle vines** on a **hot** and **sticky** morning.

This is the way we **suck** and **slurp**, **wallow** in mud, **kick** our heels.

Here we go round the waterhole on a **dry** and **dusty** morning.

This is the way we slap and clap, slip and slide, splish and splash.

Here we go round the **icicle** on a **sparkling** snowy morning.

Here we go round the mossy log on a misty moisty morning.

This is the way we **flit** and **fly**, **swoop** and **soar**, big eyes wide.

Here we go round the starry night just before the morning.

Let's all do the mulberry whoosh and mulberry swoosh mulberry swoosh around that bush!

Let's all do the **mulberry whoosh** every single morning!